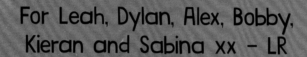

For Leah, Dylan, Alex, Bobby,
Kieran and Sabina xx – LR

For Owen, Ralph and Ruben – M.B.

Published in the UK by Scholastic, 2022
Euston House, 24 Eversholt Street, London, NW1 1DB
Scholastic Ireland, 89E Lagan Road, Dublin Industrial Estate,
Glasnevin, Dublin, D11 HP5F

SCHOLASTIC and associated logos are trademarks and/or
registered trademarks of Scholastic Inc.

Text © Lucy Rowland, 2022
Illustrations © Mike Byrne, 2022

The right of Lucy Rowland and Mike Byrne to be identified
as the author and illustrator of this work has been asserted by them
under the Copyright, Designs and Patents Act 1988.

HB ISBN 978 0702 31461 2
PB ISBN 978 0702 31361 5

A CIP catalogue record for this book is available from the British Library.

Printed in China
Paper made from wood grown in sustainable forests and other controlled sources

1 3 5 7 9 10 8 6 4 2

www.scholastic.co.uk

UNiCORNS DON'T Love SPARKLES

LUCY
ROWLAND

MIKE
BYRNE

SCHOLASTIC

Hello! I'm a **unicorn**,

but as you can see,

my unicorn friends are
quite **different** to me.

I do **NOT** love pink. **Nope!**

No **flowers** or **hearts!**

I'm **not** a big fan
of bright **unicorn** farts.

I really hate **rainbows** (I've said it before), but there are some things I dislike **even** more...

I do **NOT** love **sparkles.**

It just feels so ROTEN
to have itchy glitter
stuck right up your bottom.

It gets in your **nostrils!**

It gets in your **hair!**

And soon there is **sparkly** dust

EVERYWHERE!

I do not love balloons and the way that they

POP!

Or strange balloon animals –
please make it stop!

They bounce on the floor
and they float through the air,

they stick to your clothes
and then mess up
your hair!

I do **NOT** love sweet food.

No, I'd prefer peas.

Or maybe some broccoli

covered in cheese?

I do **not** love ice cream
or sprinkles or jelly –
who wants that stuff
wobbling round in their belly?

I do **not** like games. Nope!
No matter the weather –
no running or jumping
or "working together".

Though sometimes I DO rather like to play chess.
So, nice quiet games can be alright...I guess.

But...

I do **NOT** love presents, or maybe I would
if only my friends could pick out something good?

But all their unwrapping of fluffy pink stuff…

Well! After a while,
I've just had enough!

But now it's... my BIRTHDAY!
My head starts to spin.

A day filled with SPARKLES!
With ALL THESE THINGS IN!

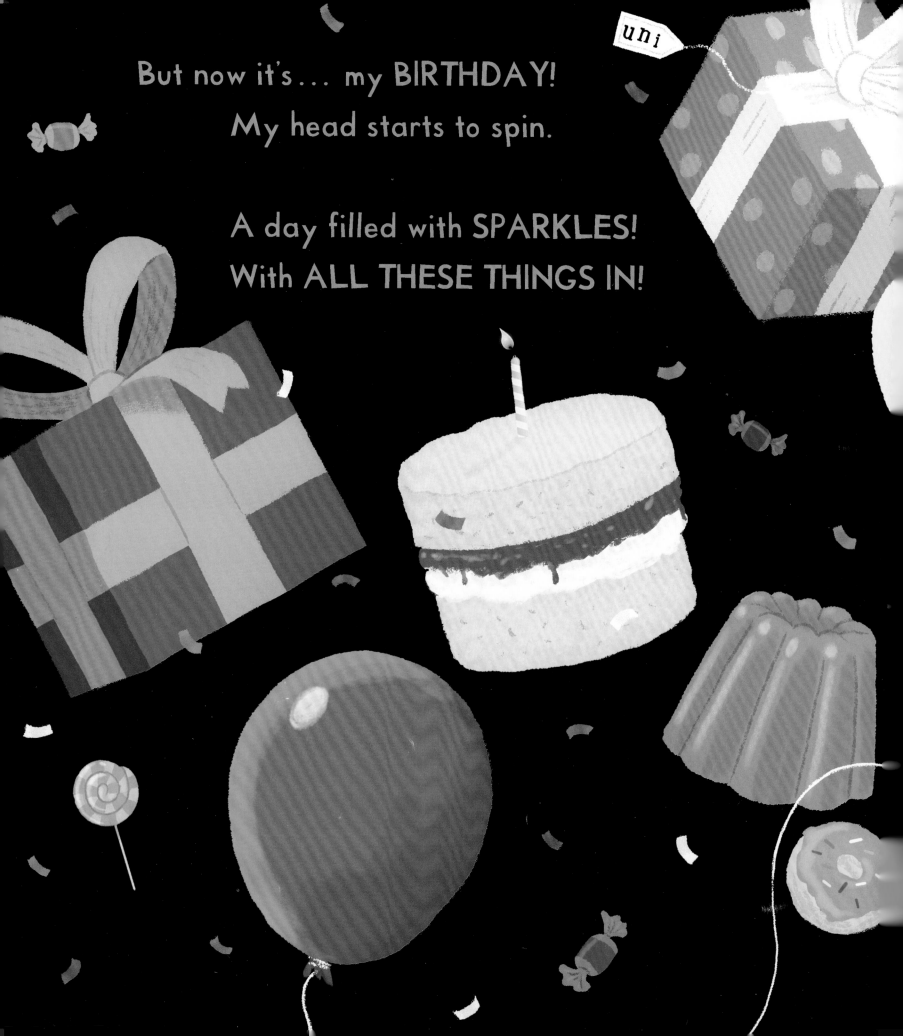

Ugh! Sweet food and sponge cake –
with candles to blow –
balloons, games and presents
and glitter . . .

OH NO!

Though, maybe, a friend or two...
that could be good?

Perhaps I should call them.
Yes, maybe I should?

I know there's no party games,
glitter or prizes...
But...

DING-DONG!

What's that?

I do **NOT** like

surprises!

"SURPRISE!"

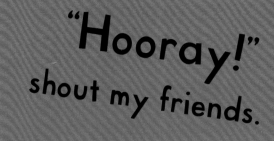

"Hooray!"
shout my friends.

"Happy Birthday!"
they cheer.

"A day just for you!
The BEST day
of the year!"

I stare at my friends –
they have dressed to **impress**.

And look! They've brought **games!**
"Yes, we thought
we'd play **chess**."

"We know that you really hate jelly and sweets,
but – here! – we've made these tasty **broccoli** treats."

No glitter, no balloons.
I look down at the plate.

My friends are so kind.
Yes, they're really
quite great!

I still don't love **sparkles** or **unicorn poo**.
And I DON'T love **birthdays**…

Or maybe I do?